MISTY'

MISCHIEF

R

Rod Campbell

VIKING KESTREL

This is Misty.
She finds lots to
do every day!

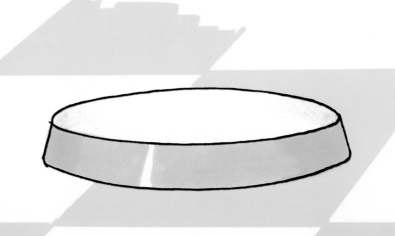

Sometimes she

chases the wool.

Sometimes she

creeps up on the birds.

Sometimes she

climbs trees.

Sometimes she

jumps

over the garden wall.

Sometimes she

plays with the kittens.

Sometimes she

teases the dog.

Sometimes she

runs in for her supper.

But she always

likes to